S0-DJW-532

I HAVE BEEN SEXUALLY ABUSED.

NOW WHAT?

JENNIFER CULP

ROSEN
PUBLISHING®

New York

Published in 2015 by The Rosen Publishing Group, Inc.
29 East 21st Street, New York, NY 10010

Copyright © 2015 by The Rosen Publishing Group, Inc.

First Edition

Library of Congress Cataloging-in-Publication Data

Culp, Jennifer.
I have been sexually abused. Now what?/Jennifer Culp.— First edition.
    pages cm.—(Teen life 411)
Includes bibliographical references and index.
ISBN 978-1-4777-7976-7 (library bound)
1. Sexually abused teenagers—Juvenile literature. 2. Sexually abused teenagers—Rehabilitation—Juvenile literature. 3. Sexual abuse victims—Juvenile literature. I. Title.
RJ507.S49C85 2015
618.92'85836—dc23
                                                                    2014011044

Manufactured in China

CONTENTS

Sexual abuse of children, preteens, and teenagers is shockingly common. Child sexual abuse is underreported and grossly under-prosecuted, but research and education are helping to change that. In the past, it was often thought that claims of sexual abuse were made up or that false memories of abuse were implanted in children by mental health professionals. Another widespread myth related to sexual abuse is the "cycle of abuse," the notion that people who were sexually abused as children grow up to become abusers themselves. Both of these ideas are false. It is incredibly rare for young people to fabricate stories of sexual abuse; in fact, survivors are far more likely to lie and claim that they *haven't* been abused when, in fact, they have. Current research shows that the cycle of abuse is a myth, too. The huge majority of abuse survivors do not grow up to perpetuate abuse themselves, and most perpetrators were not sexually abused in the past.

If you have been sexually abused, it doesn't mean that there is something wrong with you or that you deserved the abuse. Sexual abuse is the fault of no one but the perpetrator.

So what's true about sexual abuse? For starters, the vast majority of sexual abuse victims under the age of eighteen know and trust the perpetrator before being abused. "Stranger danger" is rare; sexual abuse is far more likely to be committed by a parent, step-parent, teacher, coach, close family friend, or even a teenager or kid who is friends with or related to the victim. Because of this and other factors, such as the way the brain reacts in response to trauma, it can be very difficult for sexual abuse survivors to come forward and disclose their abuse. Sometimes a phe-nomenon called dissociation occurs, where, in order to protect itself, the victim's brain separates from her body during instances of abuse, making her feel as though she is somewhere else. This typically leaves the survivor with no memory of the abuse, until it reemerges later in life in the form of scary flashbacks or sensory memories. Sexual abuse is traumatizing and may lead to further long-term symptoms such as anxiety, depression, post-traumatic stress disorder, eating disorders, and alcohol or drug abuse. Sexual abuse is known to increase suicidal thoughts and self-harming behaviors.

Sexual abuse is one of the most awful things one human being can do to another, but it doesn't have to break you. When it comes to describing people who have been sexually abused, the term "survivor" is preferred over "victim" because that's what you are: if you have lived through sexual abuse, you have survived something terrible and you are still standing. If you have been sexually abused, someone has done something awful to hurt you, but it does not mean that you are broken. It doesn't mean that you deserve bad things or that it was your fault (being sexually abused is never your fault). It doesn't mean that there is anything wrong with you, and it doesn't mean that you are doomed to a dark, dysfunctional life. Like countless others who have gone before you, you can seek help, and you can heal from the pain and hurt someone else inflicted on you.

SEXUAL ABUSE: THE FACTS

The term "child sexual abuse" encompasses any action perpetrated on a minor with the intent of arousing the perpetrator in a sexual fashion. That doesn't mean that this kind of abuse happens only to very young children. The inclusion of the word "child" merely distinguishes the fact that the abuse happened to someone under the age of eighteen.

Sexual abuse can happen to infants, very small children, preteens, and teenagers. It may take different forms: verbal, voyeuristic, touching, or some combination of all three.

Sexual abuse may be committed by a stranger, but it is far more likely to be committed by someone the survivor knows, such as a teacher, coach, parent, or relative. In fact, more than 90 percent of sexual abuse victims under the age of twelve know the perpetrator, who is often a family member. When it comes to sexual assault victims between the ages of twelve and eighteen, more than 80 percent have a prior relationship with the perpetrator.

In total, about 44 percent of all reported rape victims in the United States are under the age of eighteen. Though child sexual abuse is most often committed by adult offenders, it may also be committed by a teenager or even a

Sexual abuse is often committed by an adult the survivor knows well, which can make it very difficult to trust others. The help of caring, qualified professionals and loved ones, however, is vital to healing.

kid. Teenage girls between the ages of sixteen and nineteen are a particularly vulnerable population, being four times more likely than the general population to become victims of rape, attempted rape, or sexual assault.

YOU ARE NOT ALONE

In all cases, regardless of the specifics, sexual abuse is wrong. Whatever the circumstances, the perpetrator, *not* the victim, is solely at fault.

If you have been sexually abused, you are not alone. Sadly, sexual abuse of people under eighteen is common. Information provided by the Rape, Abuse & Incest National Network (RAINN) and U.S. Department of Justice statistics show that 29 percent of sexual assault and rape victims are between the ages of twelve and seventeen, and 15 percent are under the age of twelve. Further data reported by the United States Administration for Children and Families shows that more than 62,500 minors were sexually abused in 2012, and that only includes cases that were reported to Child Protective Services.

Many instances of sexual abuse go unreported, for a variety of reasons. For instance, a very young child who is sexually abused might not understand what is happening or realize he needs to ask for help. Feelings of confusion and shame could lead a teenager who has been sexually abused to keep quiet rather than risk becoming the subject of gossip.

Yet another person who has been sexually abused may be reluctant to ask for help because she fears she won't be believed, is afraid of getting in trouble, or is afraid of getting the perpetrator in trouble, especially if the abuse occurred at the hands of a loved one.

Survivors of sexual abuse often attempt to minimize or deny the abuse after it happens in order to cope. Other survivors may not even consciously remember being sexually abused due to trauma or dissociation during abuse. All of these reactions are normal.

Feelings of Shame

Perpetrators of sexual abuse on people under eighteen are more likely to use means other than force to coerce their victims into cooperating, such as emotional manipulation, intimidation, or supplying their target with drugs or alcohol. Thus, survivors can often be plagued by feelings of guilt, shame, and confusion. Feeling as if you didn't "fight back" or that you "went along with" the abuse can make you feel complicit in the act or make you worry that it wasn't a "real" assault.

Experiencing physical pleasure during the act of abuse can also give survivors the false impression that they must have been willing or "wanted it." In the case of teenage victims, sometimes it's even more complicated: a teenager *could* want to have sex with an adult, and even enjoy it, but that doesn't mean

it's OK or that the perpetrator didn't commit a crime. In this case, even if the victim initiates sexual overtures, the responsibility to say no and behave appropriately falls to the adult in the scenario.

Abusers often manipulate their victims using the bonds of love and trust. This causes deep trauma and confusion. It's tough to sort out your feelings when someone you care about and respect, such as a close friend, mentor, or parent, does something awful to you. Many people who experience sexual assault attempt to minimize the gravity of their own experience or deny that it was really rape or sexual assault. This sort of

If you were doing something you weren't supposed to when you were assaulted, such as drinking or doing drugs, it does not mean that you were complicit in your own abuse, or "asking for it."

justification and rationalization is a very, very common reaction to the experience of sexual abuse. If this sounds like your experience, you should know that it's normal; it's just how your brain tries to protect you in the aftermath of trauma.

Sexual Abuse's Scars

The negative effects of sexual abuse are varied and affect survivors deeply. Sexual abuse can cause long-term symptoms such as post-traumatic stress disorder, anxiety, depression, sleep disturbances, pervasive fear, difficulty with healthy sexual and emotional relationships, eating disorders, and drug and alcohol abuse.

Sexual abuse might not cause lasting physical injury, but it can leave lasting mental and emotional scars. This does not mean, however, that people who have been sexually abused are "damaged" or lesser than those who haven't. It doesn't mean that survivors are weak or broken. It does not mean that survivors of sexual abuse are doomed to lead tortured lives or that they are destined to perpetrate abuse on others.

As seventeen-year-old Jonathan, a survivor of sexual abuse at the age of thirteen, says in the book *Strong at the Heart: How It Feels to Heal from Sexual Abuse*, "Things can get better. Things can always get better. But you've got to make it happen." If you have been sexually abused, you are not alone. You can get help. You can heal. You can have—and you deserve to have—a healthy, happy life.

Keeping the experience of sexual abuse a secret is a huge burden. Confiding in a qualified, trustworthy professional and getting help can improve the situation immensely.

What "Counts" as Sexual Abuse?

A common problem encountered by survivors of sexual abuse is that other people often attempt to rationalize, downplay, or dismiss acts of sexual abuse in order to shield themselves from uncomfortable facts or even defend the perpetrator of the abuse. This is incredibly hurtful and confusing to those who have suffered sexual abuse. After living through such a thing, you may struggle to accept your own feelings and memories as legitimate, or you may wonder if your experience really "counts" as abuse.

So what does "count"? Sexual abuse can take many forms, but be aware if someone engages in any of the following:

- obscene verbal comments, in person or over the phone or Internet

Inappropriate comments, unsolicited pictures of private parts, pressuring you for compromising pictures or information—all of these fall under the umbrella of sexual abuse. You don't have to be touched physically to be violated.

- making you watch pornography or participate in "hands-off" sexual activities

ON THE WAY TO OK

"First let me say this: I am so, so sorry about what happened to you. What might still be happening to you."

Writer Sady Doyle, founder of the website Tiger Beatdown, is a survivor of sexual assault. In "We're Called Survivors Because We're Still Here" (available in full at http://www.rookiemag.com/2012/01/survivors), written to and for other survivors, Doyle emphasizes, "You are not alone in this." Though the experience of sexual abuse often leaves survivors feeling isolated, it is in fact frighteningly common ("one-in-four girls-level common," as Doyle puts it) and is never deserved. Learning that others have experienced the same sort of trauma, survived, and healed can be a very important step. You are not the only person this awful thing has happened to. You are not alone.

Often, confusion accompanies the aftermath of sexual assault. Attempting to rationalize the experience as something other than rape is very common and understandable. As Doyle writes, "forced sex and molestation are so scary that your brain often refuses to fully acknowledge them." If you think you may have been sexually assaulted, or if you would call what happened to you sexual assault if it happened to someone else, according to Doyle, you should talk to a doctor or call a rape crisis hotline. It is vitally important to locate a source of support, particularly someone with understanding of and experience with sexual abuse.

Throughout the article, Doyle is open about the fact that, after living through sexual assault, every survivor will experience pain. Relying on alcohol and drugs won't erase the hurt, and self-harm and suicide are bad solutions to the problem. "Pain is a message," Doyle writes. "What it says is: 'I want to live. Get me out of this.' Don't ever try to shut that voice up."

Eventually, with help, support, and—most importantly—time, things will get better. The pain will ease. The wounds will heal. Life will be OK. In closing, Doyle talks about the term "survivor" and what it really means for those who have lived through the horror of sexual assault: "What it means is that you faced down something that no one should ever have to. And that even this terrible thing was not enough to stop you. What it means is that you are incredibly strong."

- fondling, stroking, touching, or kissing you in a sexual fashion
- manipulating or forcing you to touch him or her in a sexual manner
- voyeurism (such as watching while you're changing, using the restroom, or taking a bath)
- exhibitionism (being deliberately naked or sexual in front of you)
- genital stimulation (either performing it on you or making you do it to him or her)
- oral, vaginal, or anal penetration with an object or any body part

As writer and sexual assault survivor Sady Doyle puts it, "If someone touched your genitals or your anus with any part of their body, or any object, without your permission, that's sexual assault. If someone touched, kissed, or fondled any part of your body without your permission, that's sexual assault. If someone threatened to get you in trouble or hurt you unless you did something sexual with them, that's sexual assault. If someone did something sexual to you when you were unable to resist—if you were trapped, or unconscious, or very drunk or high and hence not able to understand or control what was happening—that's sexual assault."

Sexual abuse may occur just once or many times repeatedly over an extended period. The nature and/ or frequency of the abuse may escalate over time. If you feel partially responsible for the continuation of abuse because you haven't told, remember that it's not your fault. Blame lies solely with the perpetrator, not the victim, and anyone who tells you otherwise is not acting in your best interest.

Is There a Profile?

There is no such thing as a stereotypical sexual abuser. Individual perpetrators of sexual abuse exist across the spectra of age, gender, ethnicity, and sexual orientation. Perpetrators in the stories of the survivors profiled in the book *Strong at the Heart* include a priest, a high school classmate, a grandmother, a cousin, a stepfather, a father, and a complete stranger.

A sexual abuser might be poor and uneducated, a

In 1977, famous film director Roman Polanski pled guilty to the charge of unlawful sex with a minor. Sadly, money and power allowed him to avoid legal punishment for his crime: he fled to France, where he still resides.

famous film director, a football coach, or an R&B singer. This is not to suggest that sexual abuse should be feared from all people, but rather to emphasize that there is no one type of "legitimate" sexual abuse, no single type of abuser or situation that "counts" as abuse. Instead, sexual abuse is committed by a wide variety of people from all walks of life, and it is perpetrated upon children,

preteens, and adolescents from all backgrounds.

In a behavioral analysis of child molesters provided by the National Center for Missing & Exploited Children, former FBI supervisory special agent Kenneth Lanning discusses the nature of child sex abusers and the problems with society's perception of the crime and its perpetrators: "In the United States during the early 21st century the term most commonly used to refer to any adult who sexually victimizes a child is predator. Many child molesters are certainly predatory in their behavior, but the widespread use of this term can be unfortunate and counterproductive," he writes.

Just as there is no stereotypical perpetrator of sexual abuse, there is no stereotypical survivor. Through no fault of their own, girls and boys from infancy to age eighteen may suffer child sexual abuse.

"Some child molesters are described as 'nice guys' not because they are successfully disguising their true wickedness but because overall they actually are nice. [...] If the term 'predator' is used, any discussion should clearly include the possibility such predators may regularly practice their faith, work hard, be kind to neighbors, love animals, and help children."

COPING

The stigma of sexual abuse can make it difficult to disclose. It feels humiliating to be violated in that way, and it can feel violating all over again to give voice to the experience in order to tell someone else about it. It is not at all uncommon to feel dirty or unworthy of help after being sexually violated. These feelings can cause you to feel alone and even to isolate yourself from others. You might feel tainted or undeserving of love and respect.

Nothing could be further from the truth. Being sexually abused does not make you a bad person. Nor does it mean that you will be likely to hurt anyone else. In the past, it was believed that survivors of child sexual abuse were likely to become sexual abusers themselves. We now know this claim to be greatly exaggerated. While a few survivors of sexual abuse may eventually become sex offenders, causality is very complicated, and many factors contribute to the choices and actions of these individuals.

Far more survivors struggle with coping mechanisms that harm only themselves, such as alcohol and drug abuse, and many survivors go on to heal and live happy, healthy lives. Just as there is no stereotypical sexual abuser, there is no stereotypical sexual abuse victim. Sexual abuse is an awful thing that happens to normal people, to children and teenagers who have done nothing to deserve it. Though it irrevocably affects those who live through it, it does not define survivors' identities or mean that they are destined to lead unhappy, unstable, or unhealthy lives.

Sexual abuse is one of the most horrible things one human being can do to another. If you have lived through sexual abuse, you have already proven your strength. You've survived something the likes of which other people can't imagine, and you're still here.

MYTHS AND FACTS

MYTH

All sexual abuse victims are girls, and all perpetrators are men.

FACT

Girls experience a higher rate of sexual abuse than boys, according to information provided by the American Humane Association, but a significant number of boys are victimized as well. Though statistics show that men commit sexual abuse more frequently than women do, not all perpetrators of sexual abuse are men.

MYTH

Child sexual abuse victims grow up to become sexual abusers in turn, following a cycle of abuse.

FACT

This widely held bit of folklore does a great disservice to survivors of sexual abuse. Psychiatric research shows that the association between early abuse and later offending behavior is complex, and the experience of sexual abuse alone does not predispose a survivor to commit abuse on another.

MYTH

Claims of sexual abuse are often made up or implanted by suggestion.

FACT

On the contrary, it is thought that sexual abuse goes unreported in many cases. Sometimes someone who was abused at a young age does not remember the abuse until later in life. This does not invalidate these survivors' experiences or mean that their memories are false, however. Some of the methods the brain uses to protect itself from trauma can cause memories to be repressed until they surface later in life. This does not mean that survivors who recall abuse in this way are lying or that remembrance of abuse is false and implanted by hypnosis or suggestion in therapy.

CHAPTER 2

Sexual abuse is an incredibly violating experience, and unsurprisingly, it can affect mental health and behavior in a number of adverse ways. This doesn't mean that everyone who is sexually abused will react in the same way or experience the same problems, but it's important to be aware of the risks and understand how some coping mechanisms may lead to further harm.

COPING IN THE DARK

Post-traumatic stress disorder (PTSD) affects a large number of sexual abuse survivors. The National Women's Study revealed that almost one-third of rape victims suffer from PTSD within their lifetimes. Additionally, women who have been raped were found to be 6.2 times more likely to develop PTSD than others who had never been victims of crime. Survivors of sexual abuse may also be diagnosed with acute stress disorder. Post-traumatic stress disorder and acute stress are normal reactions to a traumatic event, but when they persist long term, they are no longer beneficial to the healing process and cause further pain to survivors.

Major depression is a common side effect of sexual abuse, and a study of rape victims found that one in three have considered suicide.

THE EFFECTS OF SEXUAL ABUSE

According to RAINN, victims of sexual assault are three times more likely than the general population to suffer from depression, six times more likely to develop PTSD, and four times more likely to contemplate suicide. This is not because survivors of sexual abuse are weak or flawed. Survivors are more vulnerable to depression than the average population because something awful has been done to them.

Jonathan, who was abused by a trusted Catholic priest at the age of thirteen, cut himself when the pain became too great to bear. Eventually he attempted suicide. "I took a bunch of pills that I found in the house, I went to bed and planned on never waking up again. It was just too much to take anymore," he shares in the book *Strong at the Heart*. "I didn't die, but I got real sick. I didn't tell anyone what I'd done until just last year."

Sheena, who was assaulted by an older cousin who was babysitting, credits her younger sisters with saving

If you ever feel tempted to hurt yourself, please seek help immediately. Self-harm is a common coping mechanism for survivors of sexual abuse, but it is ultimately destructive.

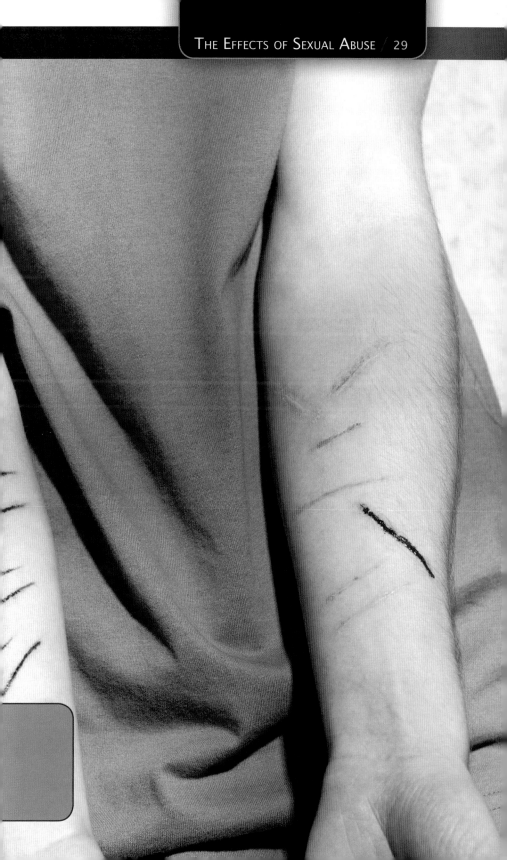

Crisis hotlines are an excellent resource during dark moments. Trained volunteers on phone and text hotlines can help survivors who feel depressed, self-destructive, or suicidal.

her from the assault (which they witnessed) and with saving her from harm at her own hands afterward. "That night, I had no hope. I felt like my life was so hard, I wanted to kill myself," she says. But then Sheena thought of her younger sisters. "I had this sudden thought: 'If I kill myself tonight, how will that make my sisters feel?' I couldn't do that to them."

TAKE BACK YOUR POWER

If you feel tempted to harm yourself or are having thoughts of suicide, call a rape crisis hotline and seek professional help right away. This is too big of a burden for any one person to carry alone, and you deserve the help of a competent professional who understands the

way you feel. Don't let the pain of what has happened to you blind you to avenues of help and healing. As Sady Doyle notes, "There is literally no one more powerless than

REACHING OUT

Breaking the silence and telling someone about what happened to you is an incredibly difficult thing to do. You might feel ashamed about what happened to you or be afraid of getting in trouble; you might worry that no one will believe you, or you may hate the idea of worrying or upsetting your loved ones. Perhaps you have been abused by a parent or guardian and feel that you have nowhere to turn.

This is where sexual abuse hotlines come in. Hotlines are staffed by professionals and trained volunteers who are experienced at dealing with all kinds of sexual abuse cases. When you call a national hotline, you are directed to speak to someone in your local area who can answer specific questions about what you should do. Most hotlines do not store your information, allowing you to ask questions anonymously. Ask up front about whether or not the counselor manning the hotline is required to report your abuse to police (many states require mandatory reporting of sexual assault of a person under the age of eighteen), and make sure you ask and understand what sort of information the hotline may gather about you before providing any details.

Calling a crisis hotline is not something to be feared. It is a way to access help and comfort without judgment. The expert advice of the hotline counselor can help you make decisions and form a strategy to tell others about the abuse. If you are anxious about the thought of talking on the phone, hotlines such as the National Sexual Assault Hotline also have online options, where you can communicate with a counselor through text chat. If you are in immediate danger, call 911.

Following are phone numbers and URLs for sexual abuse hotlines:

National Sexual Assault Hotline: (800) 656-HOPE (4673), https://ohl.rainn.org/online/
National Child Sexual Abuse Hotline: (866) FOR-LIGHT (367-5444)
Safe Horizon's Rape, Sexual Assault & Incest Hotline: (212) 227-3000
Suicide Hotline: (800) SUICIDE (784-2433)
Self Injury: (800) DON'T-CUT (366-8288)

a dead person. As long as you are alive, there is something else you can try; there is some new way you can try to take your power back. Dead people can't try anything." Hurting yourself is not productive and won't provide long-term relief. Killing yourself is not a solution. If either of these currently seems like an attractive option, please seek help immediately.

COPING WITH DRUGS AND ALCOHOL

Survivors of sexual abuse are far more likely to develop substance abuse problems than people who have not experienced sexual abuse. Like self-harm, substance abuse is a coping mechanism, a way to make the pain go away. Data provided by RAINN shows that sexual assault survivors are thirteen times more likely to abuse alcohol and twenty-six times more likely to

Drugs and alcohol may provide temporary relief from pain, but they don't solve problems. If you are tempted to drink or do drugs to cope with pain and anger, please seek help.

abuse drugs than people who have not experienced sexual abuse.

Again, this does not mean that survivors who struggle with drugs and alcohol are weak or that there is something inherently wrong with them. In the short term, substances seem like an effective way to feel better. Getting drunk or high can temporarily make you feel good, but the feeling won't last. It merely numbs the pain for a brief time, and it can make you feel even worse when you sober up again.

Abusing substances in order to feel better in the wake of sexual abuse is an understandable response, but it is ultimately unproductive and does more harm than good. Relying on drugs or alcohol to numb pain is a bad solution for adults, and it can be particularly hurtful to young people. Your brain doesn't stop developing until you reach your early twenties, and the use of mind-altering substances can impact that development permanently. You need all your strength and brainpower for the process of healing, and using alcohol and drugs robs you of that power.

If you are having trouble functioning without the help of a drug, talk to a doctor or therapist. It can be really scary to seek professional help and contemplate the thought of having what is currently your most successful coping tactic—drugs or drink—taken away from you. Far from depriving you of a coping mechanism, however, mental health professionals can provide you with much more effective tactics to deal with pain and anger.

EATING DISORDERS AS COPING MECHANISMS

Sexual abuse can also predispose survivors to eating disorders. Like drug and alcohol abuse, this is a natural response to violation. When something happens to take away your control and make you feel powerless over your own body, it's a normal response to indulge in behaviors that give you feelings of power and control over your body.

Like drug and alcohol abuse, however, disordered eating ultimately only hurts you and delays the healing process. Many people believe that girls are the only ones susceptible to eating disorders, but that is not the case. Tino, who was sexually abused by his grandmother when he was a small child, struggled with

Survivors of sexual abuse are more likely to suffer from anorexia, bulimia, disordered eating, and body dysmorphia than people who haven't suffered abuse.

alcohol abuse and anorexia as an adult. When he realized he was using alcohol dangerously, he stopped drinking but began to limit his food intake instead. "I quit drinking, but I began to starve myself," he says. "I limited myself to 800 to 1,000 calories daily and exercised two or three times a day. I went from weighing about 165 pounds right when I quit drinking to 120. I wasn't healthy, I was fanatical."

Alcohol abuse and anorexia helped Tino cope with his unresolved emotions for a time, and "kept a lid" on his memories of abuse, as he puts it. Unhealthy coping behaviors can't forestall the underlying hurt and pain forever, though; it will eventually catch up. Tino reached the point of seriously considering suicide before he sought help, when he finally called a hotline and found a qualified counselor to help him process the mental trauma that resulted from being molested as a child.

SEXUAL EFFECTS OF SEXUAL ABUSE

Unsurprisingly, sexual abuse also affects future sexual functioning. Some survivors develop issues in regard to trust and intimacy and have trouble enjoying certain sex acts or any sort of sexual touch. Engaging in particular sex acts that remind a survivor of his or her assault can trigger painful and overwhelming memories of the abuse.

It's important to communicate openly with sex partners about your experiences and personal boundaries in order to make sure that sex is a positive experience.

Someone who doesn't care if his or her actions trigger you, or who tells you that you should "get over it" or forget about your experience, is not someone who is worthy of being with you.

"You have to be willing to ask each other, 'What's this like for you? How do you feel?' And really listen. And you have to speak up for yourself as well," explains Kelly, who was abducted and raped by a stranger while walking to school at the age of fourteen. Years and years after the attack, Kelly's husband, Jason, jokingly grabbed her from behind while she was washing dishes, which triggered feelings reminiscent of being assaulted. "I was so scared. For me, it was like being grabbed by the rapist. I said, 'Don't ever do that again!' I knew he didn't mean to scare me, but he needed to know that for me it wasn't funny."

Remember, if you don't feel ready to have sex, or if the thought of sex feels scary or unpleasant, *you don't have to do it*. Even after living through sexual abuse, sex can be a positive, affirming experience with a supportive partner, but you should never feel forced or pressured into it. You are the only person who gets to decide what feels right for your own body, and you don't have to do anything you don't want to.

On the other hand, other survivors of sexual abuse react by becoming very promiscuous. You might feel that after what happened to you, what does it matter? Maybe it feels like sleeping around will make other people like you or that having voluntary sex with a bunch of people will erase the memory of being abused.

However, like drug and alcohol abuse or disordered eating, reckless sexual behavior can't erase what happened to you. At best, it postpones confronting the pain and hurt for a time. Promiscuity is a very common reaction to sexual abuse. If you react to sexual assault in this way, it doesn't mean that there is anything wrong with you or that you deserved what your abuser did to you.

Sadly, outsiders may not understand and can be very cruel, making assumptions such as "He sleeps with a lot of people, so he couldn't have been raped" or "She's a slut; she was asking for it." This sort of attitude is callous, counterproductive, and born of ignorance. Don't pay

It can be hard for other people to understand the effects of sexual abuse, and sometimes they say callous, hurtful things. Don't let someone else's ignorance affect your sense of self-worth and value.

attention to people who say something like this to you. They're wrong.

You should, however, seek professional counseling in order to better understand why you feel the way you feel and make the choices you make. Why do you want to have sex? Does it make you feel good physically and emotionally? Do you feel that your sex partners respect and support you? If not, you may be sleeping around as an unhealthy coping mechanism. Find support and figure out what you really want before allowing anyone else to have access to your body.

DISSOCIATION

As mentioned previously, some survivors of sexual abuse don't even remember experiencing abuse until much later.

Therapy and professional counseling are vitally important in the aftermath of sexual abuse. However, that doesn't mean that every counselor will be right for you. Keep looking until you find a therapist you feel comfortable with.

Dissociation is a protective strategy in which someone disconnects and feels as though he is not present in his own body while he is experiencing sexual abuse. Akaya, who was sexually abused by her father for many years, referred to her dissociation as "going to the stars." This ability allowed her to preserve her spirit in spite of the horrors that were done to her. "It was like there was a tunnel that I could climb into and I would be somewhere some-when else," she says. "I would be in the stars. He would do whatever he needed to do. Then, when it was over, my body would signal me that I could come back. Afterward, I didn't remember what he'd done. In some ways it was like it hadn't happened."

Dissociation allowed Akaya to maintain a successful academic and social life. No one would have suspected what was happening to her at home. But "going to the stars" couldn't erase the reality of what had occurred. The dissociation prevented Akaya from having to confront her sexual abuse at the hands of her father until she was an adult, when she began to experience visceral, frightening flashbacks to memories she hadn't previously recalled. She worried that she was losing her mind. With the help of a patient, skilled therapist, however, Akaya was eventually able to make sense of the memories and focus on healing and wholeness. "There was a period of time when, if I wasn't at work, my focus was on the abuse or the healing of it. It took most of my energy," she says.

"What told me that I was going to make it, that I had turned the corner, was when I started spending more time living than healing."

If you have experienced or are experiencing frightening episodes such as flashes of sound, sight, or scent—memories of abuse that you did not previously recall—don't doubt your sanity or assume that these flashes of memory must be false. Instead, speak to a doctor as soon as possible. An experienced professional can help you make sense of what is happening to you and determine how to move forward.

CHAPTER 3

CONFRONTING SEXUAL ABUSE
AND RECLAIMING CONTROL

Every survivor of sexual abuse is different, each survivor's experience of sexual abuse is different, and the path to healing is unique to every individual. No one can overcome the trauma caused by sexual abuse without help and support, however. Reaching out for help is the first step to healing.

WHAT SHOULD I DO?

If you have just been sexually assaulted, or if the abuse occurred very recently, go straight to the hospital and ask for a sexual assault forensic exam. Don't shower or change, don't wait, but go while doctors can still collect evidence against your attacker. It takes courage to do this. To report your assault when answering questions and being poked and prodded is probably the last thing you want to do, but it is very important. The longer you wait, the less likely it is that police will be able to bring your abuser to justice.

If, for whatever reason, this isn't possible—if the abuse occurred a long time ago, if you were too intimidated to seek help immediately following the assault, if you just didn't know what to do—you need to seek help from a qualified therapist or counselor. The simplest way

A professional counselor or therapist, particularly one who specializes in treating sexual abuse survivors, can help you make sense of your feelings and make positive steps toward feeling healthy and safe.

to find out specifically what to do is to call a rape crisis hotline. Even if you are seeking help for something that happened a long time ago, the trained volunteers who work the hotline can still provide answers and help you figure out what to do. The National Sexual Assault Hotline is available 24/7 at (800) 656-HOPE. Calling the 800 number will put you in touch with a counselor at the closest rape crisis center to your location so that you can speak to someone familiar with the rape and sexual assault laws specific to your area and knowledgeable about the community resources available to you.

Calling the National Sexual Assault Hotline is confidential. The service uses the area code of your phone number to connect you to a counselor in your location, but it does not record your full phone number or name. You do not have to share your personal information if you don't want to. In many states, counselors and medical professionals are required by law to report the sexual abuse of anyone under the age of eighteen to legal authorities. Ask the counselor about this up front so that you know what sort of information he or she can share (or *must share*) with authorities before you provide any information.

Once you understand the rape-crisis counselor's responsibilities in regard to reporting a crime against you, check whether he or she is obligated to save your information or not. When you call the National Sexual Assault Hotline, it is OK to decline to share your name and phone number. The counselors will still answer your questions and provide help if you choose to remain anonymous; you are not obligated to share your info in order to receive assistance.

Don't wait until you feel comfortable referring to what happened to you as sexual abuse or sexual assault before calling a counselor. You don't have to use that terminology if you don't want to; you can use whatever vocabulary you prefer to describe what has happened to you. As discussed earlier, it is often hard to accept what has occurred in loaded terms such as "rape," "assault," or "incest" immediately after it happens, but waiting until you have processed the experience on your own before calling for help deprives you of much-needed assistance at a time when it is invaluable. As Sady Doyle writes, "Right now, you are dealing with something that can have a lot of long-term consequences, and you can't always see those consequences clearly when you're living through it. You need to be in touch with at least one person whose first priority is keeping track of you, and making sure that you are OK."

COUNSELING

Calling a rape crisis hotline is the first step on the path to healing, and if you have done so, you should be proud of yourself. As counterintuitive as it may seem, it can be really scary to ask for help! For many survivors of sexual abuse, disclosing the abuse is the most difficult step on the path to recovery. And as

It's a counselor's job to help you. You can feel confident about discussing your experiences with a professional, even before you've sorted out your own thoughts and feelings about what happened.

important as it is, seeking help is just the beginning of the healing process.

Recovery takes a dedicated effort: it can take a long time, and it requires the help of a professional. There are many different types of counseling, and different approaches (or even just a different therapist) may be more beneficial for one person than another. Body-centered therapy can help restore confidence and wholeness to someone who has been physically violated. Cognitive behavioral therapy may be a good option for a survivor who struggles with drug or alcohol abuse.

It will take research to determine what option is best for you, and it might take a few tries to find a counselor who is a good fit for you personally. Sexual abuse survivor Tammy saw three different counselors before finding someone she felt truly comfortable with. "That's something people don't realize when they go to counseling," Tammy notes. "Just because you run into one or two you don't like, it doesn't mean you should give up. Eventually you will find someone you can trust and you'll have a good relationship with them."

Peer support groups are particularly important for survivors. As molestation survivor Jonathan says of the survivor support group he attended, "It was one of the biggest healing processes for me because—therapist, family, friends—no matter how much they want to help, people do not understand how you feel unless they have gone through it, too. These people became family to me. They knew exactly what I felt." Group counseling sessions

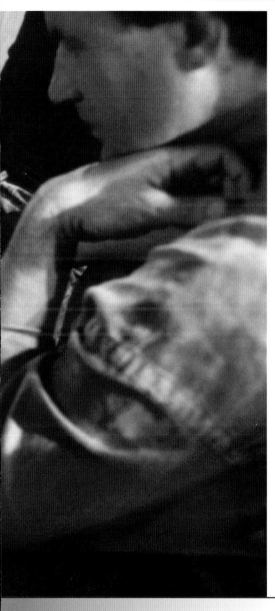

helped Tammy come to terms with what had happened to her, as well: "When the abuse was going on, I thought I was the only person in the world these things happened to and that I was to blame. It's funny, but when I heard what happened to the others, it was easier to see how it wasn't *their* fault." A local support group can be a valuable source of support. Attending group meetings plus individual counseling is a productive approach for most survivors.

Other survivors can be a great source of support; they understand what you've been through and what you're going through like no one else. If you have been sexually abused, you're not alone.

EMPOWERING LISTENERS, EMPOWERING SURVIVORS

In February 2014, Dylan Farrow wrote an open letter published by the *New York Times* in which she discussed the sexual abuse she says she suffered at the hands of her adoptive father, famed film director Woody Allen, when she was a child. It is important to note that Allen was never convicted of abusing Farrow, and some claim that Farrow was used as a pawn by her mother, actress Mia Farrow, as revenge on Allen. Even though most of the public does not know what really happened inside the Farrow-Allen household and is not in a position to make well-informed conclusions, Dylan Farrow's account ignited a firestorm of online commentary. While Farrow has legions of supporters, some of the responses to her letter revealed that many people find Allen's denial of the abuse more credible than Farrow's harrowing account of victimization at the hands of a trusted adult.

In a published response to public reception of Farrow's story, Andrea Grimes, a senior political reporter at RH Reality Check and herself an adult survivor of childhood sexual abuse, wonders, "What Would Make You Believe a Survivor of Childhood Sexual Abuse?"

"I wonder why there are so many of those kinds of people who seem unable to, simply, listen to survivors without transporting themselves into some crudely imagined, hyperbolic *Law & Order: SVU* episode full of idealized victims and nefarious abusers," Grimes writes. "I wonder how we can change that, and I believe part of the solution is to help people who aren't survivors learn to hear stories of survival in productive, non-victim-blaming ways. We need to change the paradigm of reception, to empower people to hear the words 'I was raped' or 'I was abused,' so that they can hold them and experience them without defensiveness, panic, or pity. If we do this—give listeners a cultural script for hearing these stories—I think we will go a long way toward empowering survivors to tell these stories."

"Listen to us," Grimes asks of those who have not survived sexual abuse, "so that we can listen to ourselves."

THE COMFORT OF RELIGION AND SPIRITUALITY

Many survivors, even those who aren't religious, speak of relying on spirituality to aid them throughout the healing process. Incest survivor Akaya says of her experience, "There were times when, if I hadn't had something larger than myself to rest in, I know I would not have made it."

Seventeen-year-old Jonathan lost his faith in the Catholic Church after being sexually abused by a priest,

Art and music act as positive, healing outlets for many survivors, providing a means to express difficult emotions and topics in a cathartic manner.

but he continued to rely on a higher power for strength. "I believe in God. I still pray every day," he says.

Participating in healing circles based on traditional Ojibwa healing techniques combined with modern counseling helped Sheena process her feelings after her cousin assaulted her. A first sharing circle, in which she was asked to disclose what happened in front of everyone, left Sheena feeling angry and uninterested in participating in another, but attending a second healing circle with a smaller group that focused less on the details of her assault and more about feelings helped her gain a measure of peace. "The healing circle cleared me; it gave me courage to talk to people, to tell them how I felt, and to know that it wasn't just me these things happened to," she says. Sheena's mom continues to hold family sharing circles at home to pray, talk, and listen. "My mom always asks if I'm okay. Then we close with a prayer. Those sharing circles feed my heart," Sheena says. If you aren't religious or spiritual, you don't have to seek support from those sources. If you do hold religious or spiritual beliefs of any kind, however, your faith can be a powerful source of comfort and strength throughout the healing process.

ART THERAPY

Creative endeavors such as playing music, making artwork, and writing can also help you process emotions and express yourself in meaningful ways. Jenner, who was raped by a high school classmate at age fourteen,

Playing an instrument takes investment and practice. Music not only provides a way to communicate about tough subjects but can also let you tune out and forget your worries while working on developing your skills.

felt numb about the experience for a long time. "It took years," she says in *Strong at the Heart*, "but my brain finally shut up and my emotions broke through." When that happened, Jenner locked herself in her room and began to write a song about her experience, without self-censoring or editing. "Writing that song was my catharsis," she explains. "It gave me a way to step into the experience, really feel it for the first time. It was such a relief to go ahead and feel the anger and express it in a way that was constructive."

Keeping a journal proved helpful to Tammy, allowing her not only to get her thoughts out and express them on paper, but

Making art—be it drawing, painting, music, dance, writing, or any other form of creative expression—is a powerful process in which terrible experiences and dark emotions can be used to create something wonderful.

also to look back at what she wrote later to assess how far she's come. Tino, who was sexually abused by his grandmother as a small child, says that creative expression is how he manages to deal with strong emotions. When he can't find the words to express and exorcise negative feelings, artistic expression prevents him from bottling them up.

COMMIT TO GETTING BETTER

Tenacity and commitment are imperative to healing. To get better, to feel better, you have to keep on living, even while you hurt, and keep on moving in spite of obstacles. "The decision to heal was a big decision, one I had to make almost daily," Akaya says. "It was a commitment. 'I will figure this out. I will heal from this. I will not put up with half a life. I will not!'"

According to Sady Doyle, being OK means merely that the event or events that hurt you, the terrible things that happened to you, happened a long time ago. With time, and making the choice to face what happened and move forward (over and over again if necessary), the sexual abuse that hurt you will have less and less pull over you. You'll realize that you don't think about it as often, that it just doesn't affect your daily life the way it once did. As Doyle writes, "You can get past 'OK.' You can get way past 'OK.' You can actually get to 'great.' That's where a lot of the sexual assault survivors I've met have ended up: GREAT. So

Exercise is a great coping tool for sexual abuse survivors. Using your body to achieve new feats of strength and speed boosts self-esteem, and exercise releases endorphins, which make you feel happy.

I'm not telling you that you have to be happy now. I'm telling you that it's possible, and common. And one day, you might end up there, and not even realize it until you take a second to look around."

10 Great Questions to Ask a Counselor

1. What should I do if I become overwhelmed with anxiety, panic, or fear?

2. How should I talk to my family about what happened to me?

3. What is the best way to disclose the fact that I was sexually abused to my friends?

4. How can I cope with feelings of low self-esteem or worthlessness?

5. Will I be able to have a healthy, fulfilling sexual relationship in the future?

6. What should I do if I feel tempted to physically hurt myself?

7. How can I rebuild trust and comfort in my body?

8. How can I let go of lingering feelings of hatred and anger?

9. How should I go about removing negative influences from my life and building a positive support system?

10. What sort of issues related to the abuse might come up as I age?

CHAPTER 4

In the aftermath of abuse, the people in your life who are closest to you play an invaluable role. They will be the ones to lend you strength in times of need, the people whose love and concern may keep you going when you don't feel like fighting anymore. You need loved ones in your corner. Sometimes, however, out of ignorance, fear, misdirected anger, or lack of empathy, other people can be very cruel to survivors of sexual abuse.

FACING CRUELTY

In January 2012, Daisy Coleman's mother found her fourteen-year-old daughter on the front doorstep of their house, scratching at the door in thirty-degree temperatures. Daisy's hair was frozen, and her genitals were injured. The last thing Daisy remembered from the previous night, as she shared in an article on the website XO Jane, was drinking a large glass of alcohol offered to her by Matt Barnett, a seventeen-year-old senior she'd snuck out of the house to hang out with.

Daisy was taken to the emergency room and had rape forensic evidence taken, which proved that Matt had engaged in intercourse with her. One of his friends filmed a brief video of the act with a cell phone, and the resulting footage showed

FRIENDS, FAMILY, FALLOUT

Daisy to be incoherent. Daisy's thirteen-year-old best friend, who was with her that night, was raped by a fifteen-year-old boy in another room of the same house. (This younger boy admitted to the crime, and his case was handled in the juvenile system, off the public record.)

Matt, a popular football player from a powerful local family, claimed that the sex with Daisy was consensual. In spite of the forensic evidence and the video, the charges against him were dropped. (When he was nineteen, thanks to national attention on the case, Matt made a plea deal and was convicted of the lesser charge of misdemeanor child endangerment for getting Daisy drunk and leaving her alone in the snow.)

Supporters in Maryville, Missouri, rally on behalf of Daisy Coleman, who suffered terrible community harassment after reporting that a popular local football player had raped her.

SEXUAL ABUSE AND CELEBRITIES

Child sexual abuse isn't confined to the poor and uneducated, as a Hollywood movie might have you believe, but also takes place in the world of the rich and famous.

Corey Feldman, an actor who rose to fame as a child star in the 1980s in movies such as *Gremlins*, *The Goonies*, and *The Lost Boys*, said in 2011 that pedophilia was and still is Hollywood's biggest problem and darkest secret. Feldman was sexually abused for years by his adult assistant, who plied him with drugs. Actor Corey Haim, who starred alongside Feldman in *The Lost Boys*, was raped and abused by adult men he encountered while working on movies and developed a debilitating drug addiction that eventually claimed his life in 2010. He was thirty-eight. "Corey [Haim] was raped at the age of 11," Feldman wrote of his friend in the *New York Daily News*, "and like many, many victims, drug use became an easy, if also tragic, way for him to escape the weight of that shame."

Sadly, when sexual abusers are famous, their fame and fortune can help them get away with their crimes. Decorated film director Roman Polanski has lived at large in France since 1978, when he was to be sentenced for drugging and raping a thirteen-year-old girl. Reprehensibly, many famed actors have spoken out in support of Polanski in the years since and aired their views that the charges against him should be dropped, without thought for the experience of his victim. R&B singer R. Kelly has become a bit of a pop cultural punch line in recent years over his preference for sexual relations with young teenage girls. What many people who make tasteless jokes about Kelly and teens fail to realize is that Kelly is well known as a predator who sexually abuses young black girls in the Chicago area. Though an abundance of evidence of Kelly's crimes is available on record, he was acquitted of child pornography charges (for taping himself performing explicit sex acts on a fourteen-year-old girl, when he was thirty-five) and has never been tried in a court of law for rape. "Kelly was fully capable of intimidating people. These girls feared for their lives. They feared for the safety of their families. And these people talked to me not because I'm [a] super reporter—we rang a lot of doorbells on the South and West sides, and people were eager to talk about this guy, because they wanted him to stop!" says Jim DeRogatis, who has conducted the most extensive reporting on Kelly's predation over the years. Though wealth and power have shielded abusers like Roman Polanski and R. Kelly from legal consequence, easy access to information via the Internet now allows fans who may previously have been ignorant to learn about their crimes and the harm they inflicted on their victims.

Daisy's experience, in the meantime, was hellish. She was bullied terribly at school and online. Classmates and strangers alike told her that she was "asking for it," that she deserved what was done to her, that she was a "skank" and a "liar." In the account of her story published by XO Jane, Daisy recalled seeing a girl turn up to one of her dance competitions wearing a homemade T-shirt that read "Matt 1, Daisy 0." People told her that she should kill herself, and she did try to do so, ending up in the hospital following a suicide attempt in January 2014. Eventually Daisy and her family moved about 40 miles (64 kilometers) away. According to *USA Today*, "they left as a result of harassment, bullying at school and social media attacks against the family." Their empty, unsold house in Maryville, Missouri—the town in which the events took place (where Matt and his family still live)—burned to the ground.

Daisy's story isn't mentioned here to scare you or make you feel that you shouldn't share your experiences for fear of bullying and harassment. What was done to Daisy and her family by their community following that terrible winter night is extreme. Most sexual abuse victims do not experience such horrible treatment from their communities in the aftermath of their

Other people can be callous and cruel. This doesn't mean that they're right or that your experiences are not legitimate. You deserve kindness and support.

abuse. Daisy's experience has something in common with that of every survivor of sexual abuse, however: at some point, in some way, whether out of ignorance or outright cruelty, someone else will say something awful about sexual abuse to you. Unfairly, much of the burden of educating others about the reality of sexual abuse and the harm it does has historically fallen to, and continues to fall to, survivors. This is why, according to Daisy Coleman, she went public with her story: she refuses to let others rewrite the narrative of her own experiences, to allow other people to say horrible things to and about her without consequence. "I'm different now, and I can't ever go back to the person I once was. That one night took it all away from me. I'm nothing more than just human, but I also refuse to be a victim of cruelty any longer," she writes.

Friends are a powerful source of comfort and support, but you don't have to talk about sexual abuse with them if you don't want to. Hanging out and having a good time is a healing experience in itself.

"This is why I am saying my name. This is why I am not shutting up."

LOOK FOR SUPPORT

Jonathan, who shares his experience of healing from sexual abuse in the book *Strong at the Heart*, worried that his friends would laugh at him when he first spoke

out. On the contrary, they turned out to be an unfailing source of support. Classmates he didn't know well were more difficult to deal with, however.

Out of discomfort and insecurity, some people avoided Jonathan after he spoke out about his experience. Overhearing a classmate joke about molestation in the hallway upset Jonathan greatly, but he tried to remain focused on the positive aspects that came about due to his openness. "The guy who made that comment apologized to me later," Jonathan adds. "I said, 'Don't worry about it.' If I hadn't been abused, if I'd just heard this story, I wouldn't know what to think either. I might be joking about it, too. But when people really look at what happened and get some insight, they are more understanding than you would ever think."

Jonathan feels that it was ultimately a positive, healing experience to be open about the fact that he was sexually abused. Not everyone feels that way, however, and you don't have to share your own experience with others (outside of your therapist, close loved ones, and future sex partners) if you don't want to. That's fine. You should do what feels right for you.

If you do wish to tell other people that you were sexually abused—and most survivors do wish to tell at least close friends at some point, if not the general public—you are under no obligation to provide details. You can talk about what was done to you without describing the acts of abuse. No one else is

entitled to that information unless you feel comfortable sharing it. As Jonathan says, "You don't have to
talk to all your friends about everything. You don't
have to get too much into details. It's hard to go into
those segments of the past where you're not totally
healed. The best person to do that with is a therapist."

TALKING TO YOUR FAMILY

Your therapist can also help you make the decision about
whether or not you want to talk to others about your experience, as well as help you navigate the difficult emotional
terrain of talking about your abuse with family. When it
comes to parents and siblings, communication about sexual abuse can be particularly challenging. Hopefully, your
family is loving and supportive of you. This isn't always
the case, and if your family is not a source of support
for your healing—if your abuser is one of your family
members, if family members choose not to believe you,
if your family members struggle with their own mental
health problems that make it difficult for them to help
you, whatever the case may be—you should immediately
discuss these issues with a counselor.

Even in the best possible circumstances, when your
family is a source of support to you in your healing, it
can be challenging to communicate about your experience of sexual abuse with your loved ones. Your family
members could feel guilty and upset that they weren't
able to protect you; they may feel angry and helpless at

Sexual abuse is also hurtful to survivors' families, but it is not a survivor's responsibility to heal his or her loved ones' pain. Therapy is recommended for sexual abuse survivors' parents and siblings.

not being able to take your pain away. A therapist can help you figure out the best way to talk to your family about your abuse.

Your family members might need help to resolve their own emotions and issues stemming from your abuse, as well. Your experience of sexual abuse affects not just you but those who love you, as well. Members of your family might benefit from the aid of a counselor. You should ask your counselor for guidance about this. It might be best for them to seek the help of a professional other than the one you see. Speaking with a counselor can help them process their own feelings so that they can be the best possible source of support to you. It's not your job to make your family and loved ones feel comfortable with your experience. Therapy can help everyone involved cope with what has happened, and heal.

CHAPTER 5

MOVING FORWARD

You may have noticed that many of the survivors whose experiences are discussed throughout this resource—Akaya, Dean, Sady, Andrea, Tino, and Kelly, to name a few—are adult survivors of sexual abuse. As teenage survivor Jonathan pointed out in *Strong at the Heart*, there are far more resources for survivors of child sexual abuse now than there were previously.

According to former FBI supervisory special agent Ken Lanning, society began to become more aware of the problem of child sexual abuse in the 1970s and '80s. From a historical point of view, that's not that long ago. People who are now middle-aged didn't necessarily have access to support and healing resources when they began the process of healing, and many of them may have tried to avoid confronting the issue until later in life or didn't even remember their experiences until they became adults.

But the reality is that sexual abuse wounds deeply, and healing from the abuse and its aftereffects takes a long time. Healing isn't something that happens in one run, that you finish and then it's done forever. As Sady Doyle writes for *Rookie*, the end of heartbreak doesn't come with an announcement. No one arrives on your doorstep to crown you "King

Healing takes time, and sometimes it can take a long time. Be patient with yourself, no matter how long it takes.

of Over It" to mark the end of recovery. Hurt resulting from the abuse will wax and wane, and issues relating to the abuse will affect you differently at different ages and stages of your life.

ACCUSING YOUR ABUSER

A matter that may or may not greatly impact your healing journey, depending on the specifics of your

In this image, the father of a teen found delinquent of rape and other charges apologizes to the victim and her family in court in Steubenville, Ohio, in 2013.

experience, is whether or not you pursue legal action against your abuser. Sadly, the rate of conviction for crimes of sexual assault in the United States is shockingly low. In some cases, though, perpetrators are caught and brought to justice.

Kelly, who shared the story of her rape at age fourteen in the book *Strong at the Heart*, was able to remember and record the license plate number of the man who abducted and raped her. A forensic sexual assault exam

performed immediately after the attack allowed authorities to collect evidence, and Kelly immediately wrote down everything that had happened in minute detail. The amount of evidence against the perpetrator was enough to convict, and when police went to apprehend the man, he admitted to the crime. Later it was discovered that Kelly's rapist had raped and murdered another girl previously. Kelly's testimony helped convict him of the crime, and he was sentenced to life in prison.

Kelly's story went the way such a story *should* go: Kelly's attacker was caught, prevented from hurting anyone else, and punished for his crimes. Kelly had to face him in court, to testify about the terrible thing that her attacker did to her, but she will never have to worry about seeing him on the street or be afraid that he will try to seek revenge on her for his punishment.

When Sheena's older cousin was sentenced for sexually assaulting her, however, he didn't receive jail time. Allowed to live at home, her attacker was required to attend counseling and participate in an offender program. "When he didn't get time, I started crying again," Sheena said. "I got scared he'd do something else to me. He's supposed to stay away from me, but what if I met him on the road around here? Would he beat me up?"

In cases such as Daisy Coleman's, discussed earlier, the results of going to the police turned out to be nightmarish. The older boy who drugged Coleman and left her for dead was cleared of charges of raping her, her reputation in the community suffered, and she was bullied so badly that her family moved to another city in order to escape the harassment.

Make Informed Decisions

Sometimes, as it always should, going to the police to report sexual abuse results in justice: punishing predators and keeping survivors safe. At other times, however, seeking legal recourse actually ends up putting a survivor through further trauma, sometimes— tragically—to little good purpose. This absolutely does not mean that you should automatically avoid reporting sexual abuse to law authorities or be fearful of going to the police; it merely means that you should talk to someone who can help you make informed decisions. A local rape crisis counselor, who can be contacted by calling the National Sexual Assault Hotline, can answer your questions and help you decide what course of action is best.

The outcome of legal action against your abuser can have a great impact on your healing and the rest of your life: Will he or she be sentenced to prison and removed from society or acquitted of wrongdoing due to lack of evidence? Is it possible that he or she will receive jail time and then be released from prison when you are older? Talk to, or have someone you trust to advocate for you, such as a parent, guardian,

It's important to talk to someone who can help you make informed decisions, such as a rape crisis counselor, when deciding what to do in the aftermath of sexual abuse.

or trusted adult, talk to a rape crisis counselor and ask for advice about prosecuting your abuser. As the National Sexual Assault Hotline information page says, "If you have questions and are undecided about reporting, call the National Sexual Assault Hotline at 1.800.656.HOPE. A trained hotline volunteer or staff can provide you with the information you'll need to understand the reporting process."

HEALING AND GROWING

Being subjected to sexual abuse will likely have some impact on your future sexual experiences. That doesn't mean that the abuse will shape your sexual identity— that, for example, as Jonathan worried, being abused by a member of the same sex means you're gay. Your sexuality is your own, and though living through sexual abuse might make some aspects of sex more difficult to confront than they might be for a non-survivor, the abuse does not define your sexual identity.

In the book *Strong at the Heart*, some common threads ran throughout the stories of adult survivors when the subject turned to sex: Satisfying, pleasurable sexual experiences sprang from trust, respect, and communication. This is true for anyone, but it is particularly important for survivors. Sexual abuse shouldn't stop you from exploring your sexuality, but you should be mindful that you choose a partner or

partners who respect you and make your comfort and pleasure a priority. Sex, or certain sex acts, or just being physically intimate with another person at all might be scary. Be patient with yourself, and expect no less from your partner.

Sometimes frightening memories or feelings related to sexual abuse may return or happen for the first time, even though you're already involved in a well-established, supportive sexual relationship. If this occurs, it doesn't mean there's anything wrong with you or your partner. It's merely part of the healing process. Seeking ongoing therapy for such hurtful aftereffects of abuse

Survivors of sexual abuse can absolutely have healthy sexual relationships. Be kind and considerate to yourself and make sure you have a partner you can trust and who cares about your health and safety.

is beneficial, and open, honest, nonjudgmental communication with your partner is a must.

And remember, you don't have to have sex if you don't feel 100 percent comfortable, even if you've had sex before. "When it came on my terms—when I decided I was ready—I found that sex was a really positive experience," Kelly shares in *Strong at the Heart*. Counseling for both you and your future partner is a wise strategy. As Shonna Milliken Humphrey writes for the *Atlantic*, in an essay about her experience being married to a survivor of child sexual abuse, "Partners like me have very few resources. There's no recourse, no opportunity for revenge,

Listening to yourself and honoring your own needs is vital in order to develop a strong, positive relationship. A good partner respects you and prioritizes your comfort.

or even forgiveness. My challenges are loneliness, impotence, and the urge to do something, somehow to make it right." Therapy, both singly and as a couple, can help partners of abuse survivors cope with their own feelings that arise from the experience of their loved one.

Having Children

Pregnancy can be a scary experience for women who have been sexually abused, as it causes dramatic, uncontrollable changes in the body. Additionally, the many intimate medical exams that come part and parcel with being pregnant can be distressing for a survivor. Having children is certainly possible for sexual abuse survivors, but it should be approached carefully, with the support of a counselor who is knowledgeable about the challenges that abuse survivors face in pregnancy and childbirth.

Once they're born, raising children can also present challenges for survivors that those who haven't experienced sexual abuse don't experience, not because survivors are tempted to reenact their own abuse, but because having and caring for a child may cause flashbacks or bring up long-buried or previously unearthed feelings related to the abuse. In fact, survivors may feel particularly protective and worried about shielding their own children from the same situations they themselves suffered.

Dean Trippe, rape survivor and author of the comic *Something Terrible,* writes that when he found out he

The "cycle of abuse," the old idea that people who have been sexually abused go on to abuse others in turn, is a myth. Sexual abuse survivors can go on to become great parents.

was going to have a child, he prayed for a daughter, fearing that his childhood experiences would affect his relationship with a son. "I ended up having the best and brightest son in the world, but I avoided changing diapers or helping with bath time," he writes. Dean's relationship with his son's mother didn't work out, but he was able to surmount his fears that his history of sexual abuse would taint his relationship with his son. "My son's the best thing to ever happen to me, and I wouldn't change a second of my life to not have him here."

Jonathan, still a teen, draws strength from his relationships with his nieces and nephews, particularly his one-year-old niece, Angel. "Being an uncle is cool," he says. "I definitely want to have kids someday. I'm just not ready now." You, too, can have children someday, if you want to. You should, however, remain aware of the issues pregnancy and childbirth might raise and be prepared to confront them in therapy prior to making the decision to have kids.

SOMETHING TERRIBLE

When Dean Trippe was five years old, he was threatened at gunpoint and raped by a teenage boy for three days. Fortunately, thanks to the efforts of his mother, Dean's attacker was caught and prosecuted, but Dean remained alone in a world of pain and darkness for years, until help arrived in the form of *Batman,* the 1989 movie starring Michael Keaton. Though Dean had previously enjoyed watching Batman on *Super Friends* and the original TV show starring Adam West, he had never before encountered Batman's origin story or known about the trauma that invaded Bruce Wayne's childhood before he became Batman. "It struck a chord in me that I didn't fully understand at the time," Trippe writes. "But I think it was the simple message of all good superhero stories: You are who you choose to be. It's not what happens to you that makes you who you are, but what you choose to do with it."

As Trippe grew up in the 1990s, when the myth of the "cycle of abuse" became popular on police procedural shows, he became terrified that the terrible thing that had been done to him might somehow infect him and make him become a monster in turn. He swore to take his own life if he ever had sexual thoughts about children. Again, Batman came to the rescue in the form of a comic Trippe drew, in which Batman traveled through time to save young Dean from sexual abuse and free him of the burden of fear he carried. When he learned that the majority of sexual abuse survivors do not, in fact, go on to become sexual abusers, Trippe finally felt able to set aside the invisible gun he'd held to his head since he was small.

"I was in the darkness. The story of Batman helped me realize I could wrap it around my arms like a security blanket. Or a cape. The yellow symbol on my chest was my light defended by a black creature more powerful than anything crime could throw at me. A creature of the night, something terrible. A bat," Trippe writes. The act of bringing Batman to our world, to his own past, in the comic *Something Terrible* changed Dean Trippe's story, and he shared it with the world in case it helps to change yours for the better: "If you're an adult [or teenage] survivor of sexual abuse, I made this comic just to let you know there's not something terrible lurking inside you."

SUBSTANCE ABUSE

Drug and alcohol abuse are other problems that can follow sexual abuse survivors into adulthood. As previously mentioned, sexual abuse survivors are thirteen times more likely to abuse alcohol and twenty-six times more likely to abuse drugs than the general population. Given the traumatic nature of sexual abuse, this is very understandable. In the short term, numbing the pain with drink or drugs seems like a successful solution. The reality, however, is that substance abuse doesn't solve the underlying issues. It merely pushes them off to return at a later time, while the substance does damage to the body and the mind's ability to process and heal.

If you are a sexual abuse survivor, you should be aware of the statistics regarding survivors and substance abuse and be prepared to get help if you are tempted to turn to substances as a coping mechanism. Remaining vigilant and accountable to yourself and being strong enough to seek help and support are imperative when it comes to fighting the lure of substance-induced relief. Actor Corey Haim, who waged a lifelong battle with addiction following his sexual abuse at the hands of men who gave him drugs, described himself as a "chronic relapser" to *People* magazine in 2008. "I guess I always will be," he added. Tragically,

> Moving on from the experience of sexual abuse is difficult. Like any other journey, though, it gets easier once you take the first step.

his words became self-fulfilling prophecy when he died of an overdose in 2010, at the age of thirty-eight.

Sexual abuse is a far-reaching crime. The experience of living through sexual abuse will affect you throughout your life, in different ways and at different times, but the experience does not define you or dictate your life's path. It is one of many experiences that will shape the person you come to be. You have already shown yourself to be strong, and brave, because you are still here. You have lived through the unthinkable, and you are searching for answers to help you heal. With the courage and determination you already possess, you—for the rest of your life—will continue to move forward, and as you do so, your life will continue to get better.

GLOSSARY

anxiety Nervous disorder characterized by a state of excessive uneasiness and apprehension, usually with compulsive behavior and/or panic attacks.

body dysmorphia Excessive concern about and preoccupation with a self-perceived defect in physical appearance, which may not actually exist.

child sexual abuse Any action done to someone under the age of eighteen for the purpose of sexually arousing and satisfying the perpetrator.

coercion When a perpetrator uses means other than force, such as intimidation, bribery, or emotional manipulation in order to convince the victim to cooperate.

coping mechanism A conscious or unconscious behavior undertaken to help someone regain a sense of comfort and control following trauma.

cycle of abuse The myth that people who are sexually abused as children are likely to become sexual abusers themselves in adulthood.

depression Severe despondency and dejection, often accompanied by feelings of hopelessness and inadequacy.

disclosure To tell someone about the experience of sexual abuse.

dissociation When the mind separates itself and becomes unaware of the body, usually in response to extreme physical and/or emotional trauma.

eating disorder A range of psychological disorders characterized by abnormal or disturbed eating habits.

incest Sexual activity between closely related family members.

perpetrator Someone who forces or coerces a minor into engaging in sexual activity.

post-traumatic stress disorder An anxiety disorder that may develop after a person is exposed to one or more traumatic events.

predator Another term for perpetrator.

RAINN The Rape, Abuse & Incest National Network, the largest anti-sexual assault organization in the United States.

rape A type of sexual assault, often defined by penetrative action, that one or more people perpetrate on someone without his or her consent.

rape crisis hotline A group of counselors and trained volunteers who are available to offer help to sexual assault victims over the phone or Internet.

repress To attempt to push away unwanted memories or feelings, either consciously or unconsciously.

self-harm The act of deliberately injuring one's own body, not as a suicide attempt, but as a coping mechanism to deal with emotional pain, anger, and frustration.

sexual assault Sexual activity that is forced upon or coerced out of someone without his or her explicit consent.

sexual harassment Unwanted sexual advances or obscene remarks.

substance abuse Overindulgence in or dependence on an addictive substance, especially alcohol or drugs.

survivor Someone who has lived through the experience of sexual abuse.

trigger A topic that may bring about disturbing memories or flashbacks for a survivor.

victim Someone who has been sexually abused; the preferred terminology is "survivor."

voyeurism Sexual interest in spying on people engaged in intimate behaviors, such as bathing, using the restroom, or changing clothes.

FOR MORE INFORMATION

MaleSurvivor
4768 Broadway, #527
New York, NY 10034
Website: http://www.malesurvivor.org

MaleSurvivor provides resources to male survivors of sexual trauma and all their partners in recovery by building communities of hope, healing, and support.

Pandora's Project
3109 W. 50th Street, Suite #320
Minneapolis, MN 55410
(612) 234-4204
Website: http://www.pandorasproject.org

Pandora's Project, founded in 1999, provides information, support, and resources to survivors of rape and sexual abuse, as well as their friends and family.

RAINN (Rape, Abuse, & Incest National Network)
2000 L Street NW, Suite 505
Washington, DC 20036
(202) 544-1034
National Sexual Assault Hotline: (800) 656-HOPE (4673)
Website: http://www.rainn.org

RAINN is the United States' largest anti-sexual violence organization. RAINN created and operates the National Sexual Assault Hotline (800-656-HOPE and online.rainn.org) in partnership with more than

1,100 local rape crisis centers across the country and operates the DoD Safe Helpline for the Department of Defense. RAINN also carries out programs to prevent sexual violence, help victims, and ensure that rapists are brought to justice.

Safe Horizon
2 Lafayette Street, 3rd Floor
New York, NY 10007
1 (800) 621-HOPE (4673)
Website: http://www.safehorizon.org/index.php
Safe Horizon provides comprehensive support for victims of domestic violence, child abuse, human trafficking, rape, and sexual assault, as well as homeless youth and families of homicide victims.

Toronto Rape Crisis Centre
P.O. Box 84, Station B
Toronto, ON M5T 2T2
Canada
(416) 597-8808
Website: http://www.trccmwar.ca
This is a grassroots, women-run collective working toward a violence-free world by providing anti-oppressive, feminist peer support to survivors of sexual violence through support, education, and activism.

Victoria Sexual Assault Centre
#201-3060 Cedar Hill Road
Victoria, BC, V8T 3J5
Canada
(250) 383-5545
Website: http://www.vsac.ca

The Victoria Sexual Assault Centre is a feminist organization committed to ending sexualized violence through healing, education, and prevention. It is dedicated to supporting women and all trans survivors of sexual assault and childhood sexual abuse, through advocacy, counseling, and empowerment.

Washington Coalition of Sexual Assault Programs (WCSAP)

4317 6th Avenue SE, Suite 102

Olympia, WA 98503

(360) 754-7583

Website: http://www.wcsap.org

WCSAP provides information, training, and expertise to programs and individuals who support victims, family and friends, the general public, and all those whose lives have been affected by sexual assault.

WEBSITES

Because of the changing nature of Internet links, Rosen Publishing has developed an online list of websites related to the subject of this book. This site is updated regularly. Please use this link to access the list:

http://www.rosenlinks.com/411/Sexu

FOR FURTHER READING

Andersen, Laurie Halse. *Speak*. New York, NY: Square Fish (reprint), 2011.

Bass, Ellen. *Beginning to Heal: A First Book for Survivors of Child Sexual Abuse*. New York, NY: Perennial, 1993.

Blount, Patty. *Some Boys*. Naperville, IL: Sourcebooks Fire, 2014.

Bromley, Nicole Braddock. *Breathe: Finding Freedom to Thrive in Relationships After Childhood Sexual Abuse*. Chicago, IL: Moody Publishers, 2009.

Bromley, Nicole Braddock. *Hush: Moving from Silence to Healing After Childhood Sexual Abuse*. Chicago, IL: Moody Publishers, 2007.

Caplin, Sarahbeth. *Someone You Already Know*. Houston, TX: Halo Publishing International, 2012.

Carpenter, Erin. *Life, Reinvented: A Guide to Healing from Sexual Trauma for Survivors and Loved Ones*. Carnforth, England: Quantum Publishing, 2014.

Clayton, Colleen. *What Happens Next*. New York, NY: Little, Brown and Company, 2012.

Davis, Laura. *Allies in Healing: When the Person You Love Was Sexually Abused as a Child*. New York, NY: William Morrow Paperbacks, 1991.

Dessen, Sarah. *Just Listen*. New York, NY: Speak, 2008.

Deuker, Carl. *Swagger*. New York, NY: Houghton Mifflin Harcourt Publishing Company, 2013.

Feuereisen, Patti. *Invisible Girls: The Truth About Sexual Abuse*. Emeryville, CA: Seal Press, 2009.

Friedman, Jaclyn, and Jessica Valenti. *Yes Means Yes!: Visions of Female Sexual Power and a World Without Rape*. Emeryville, CA: Seal Press, 2008.

Goobie, Beth. *The Dream Where the Losers Go*. Montreal, Canada: Orca Book Publishers, 2006.

Hoover, Colleen. *Hopeless*. Amazon Digital Services, Inc., 2012.

Hunter, Mic. *Abused Boys: The Neglected Victims of Sexual Abuse*. Lexington, MA: Lexington Books, 1990.

Klein, Alina. *Rape Girl*. South Hampton, NH: Namelos, 2012.

Lew, Mike. *Victims No Longer: The Classic Guide for Men Recovering from Sexual Child Abuse*. New York, NY: Harper Perennial, 2004.

Lyga, Barry. *Boy Toy*. New York, NY: Houghton Mifflin Company, 2007.

Maltz, Wendy. *The Sexual Healing Journey: A Guide for Survivors of Sexual Abuse*. New York, NY: William Morrow, 2012.

Mather, Cynthia. *How Long Does It Hurt? A Guide to Recovering from Incest and Sexual Abuse for*

Teenagers, Their Friends, and Their Families. San Francisco, CA: Jossey-Bass, 2004.

Maybury, Deb. *Unlock The Door—Beyond Sexual Abuse.* Seattle, WA: Amazon Digital Services, Inc., 2013.

Rainfield, Cheryl. *Scars.* Lodi, NJ: WestSide Books, 2010.

Randis, K.L. *Spilled Milk: Based on a True Story.* Seattle, WA: Amazon Digital Services, Inc., 2013.

Sapphire. *Push.* New York, NY: Knopf, 1996.

Scott, Mindi. *Live Through This.* New York, NY: Simon & Schuster, 2012.

Sebold, Alice. *Lucky: A Memoir.* New York, NY: Scribner, 2002.

Stevens, Courtney. *Faking Normal.* New York, NY: HarperTeen, 2014.

Walker, Alice. *The Color Purple.* New York, NY: Harcourt Brace Jovanovich, 1982.

Warner, Ashley. *The Year After: A Memoir.* CreateSpace Independent Publishing Platform, 2013.

Young, Chris. *Uncovering Buried Child Sexual Abuse: Healing Your Inner Child and Yourself.* Tailor-Made Books, LLC, 2013.

BIBLIOGRAPHY

Caulfield, Phillip. "Missouri Teen at Center of
    Explosive Rape Case Attempts Suicide: Report."
    New York Daily News, January 7, 2014. Retrieved
    March 5, 2014 (http://www.nydailynews.com/
    news/national/missouri-teen-explosive-rape-case
    -attempts-suicide-report-article-1.1568435).
Child Maltreatment 2012. Administration on Children,
    Youth and Families of the U.S. Department of
    Health and Human Services, 2012. Retrieved
    February 25, 2014 (http://www.acf.hhs.gov/sites/
    default/files/cb/cm2012.pdf).
"Child Sexual Abuse." American Humane
    Association, 2013. Retrieved March 7, 2014
    (http://www.americanhumane.org/children/
    stop-child-abuse/fact-sheets/child-sexual
    -abuse.html).
Coleman, Daisy. "I'm Daisy Coleman, the Teenager
    at the Center of the Maryville Rape Media Storm,
    and This Is What Really Happened." XO Jane,
    October 18, 2013. Retrieved March 7, 2014
    (http://www.xojane.com/it-happened-to-me/
    daisy-coleman-maryville-rape).
Doyle, Sady. "We're Called Survivors Because
    We're Still Here." *Rookie,* January 6, 2012.
    Retrieved March 1, 2014 (http://www.rookiemag
    .com/2012/01/survivors).

"Facts About Sex Offenders." State of California Department of Justice, Office of the Attorney General, 2009. Retrieved February 25, 2014 (http://www.meganslaw.ca.gov/facts.aspx).

Farrow, Dylan. "An Open Letter from Dylan Farrow." *New York Times,* February 1, 2014. Retrieved March 5, 2014 (http://kristof.blogs.nytimes .com/2014/02/01/an-open-letter-from-dylan -farrow).

Glasser, M., I. Kolvin, et al. "Cycle of Child Sexual Abuse: Links Between Being a Victim and Becoming a Perpetrator." *British Journal of Psychiatry,* December 2001. Retrieved March 3, 2014 (http:// bjp.rcpsych.org/content/179/6/482.full).

Grimes, Andrea. "What Would Make You Believe a Survivor of Childhood Sexual Abuse?" RH Reality Check, February 4, 2014. Retrieved March 5, 2014 (http://rhrealitycheck.org/ article/2014/02/04/make-believe-survivor -childhood-sexual-abuse).

Hilton, M.R., and G.C. Mezey. "Victims and Perpetrators of Child Sexual Abuse." *British Journal of Psychiatry,* October 1996. Retrieved March 3, 2014 (http://www.academia.edu/ 1144865/Victims_and_Perpetrators_of_Child _Sexual_Abuse).

Hopper, Jessica. "Read the 'Stomach-Churning' Sexual Assault Accusations Against R. Kelly in Full." *Village Voice,* December 16, 2013.

Retrieved March 7, 2014 (http://blogs
.villagevoice.com/music/2013/12/read_the
_stomac.php).

Humphrey, Shonna Milliken. "On Marrying
a Survivor of Childhood Sexual Abuse."
Atlantic, August 27, 2013. Retrieved March
9, 2014 (http://www.theatlantic.com/health/
archive/2013/08/on-marrying-a-survivor-of
-childhood-sexual-abuse/278967).

"Info for Survivors." RAINN, 2012. Retrieved
March 9, 2014 (https://ohl.rainn.org/online/
resources/info-for-survivors.cfm).

Kilpatrick, Dean G. "The Mental Health Impact
of Rape." National Violence Against Women
Prevention Research Center, Medical University
of South Carolina, 2000. Retrieved February 27,
2014 (https://www.musc.edu/vawprevention/
research/mentalimpact.shtml).

Lanning, Kenneth V. *Child Molesters: A Behavioral
Analysis, for Professionals Investigating the Sexual
Exploitation of Children.* National Center for
Missing & Exploited Children, 2010. Retrieved
March 1, 2014 (http://www.missingkids.com/
en_US/publications/NC70.pdf).

Lehman, Carolyn. *Strong at the Heart: How It Feels
to Heal from Sexual Abuse.* New York, NY:
Melanie Kroupa Books, 2005.

"National Sexual Assault Hotline - 1.800.656.
HOPE." RAINN, 2009, Retrieved March

1, 2014 (http://www.rainn.org/get-help/
national-sexual-assault-hotline).

Sieczkowski, Cavan. "Corey Feldman's 'Coreyography'
Details Sexual Abuse He, Corey Haim Faced."
Huffington Post, October 21, 2013. Retrieved March
9, 2014 (http://www.huffingtonpost.com/2013/10/21/
corey-feldman-sexual-abuse_n_4136524.html).

Trippe, Dean. *Something Terrible.* 2013. Retrieved
February 10, 2014 (deantrippe.com).

"Who Are the Victims?" RAINN. 2009. Retrieved
March 1, 2014 (http://www.rainn.org/get
-information/statistics/sexual-assault-victims).

INDEX

ABOUT THE AUTHOR

Jennifer Culp is an author and former editorial coordinator for the *Southern Medical Journal* and managing editor for the *Journal of Clinical Densitometry*. She writes nonfiction for young adults and children.

PHOTO CREDITS